50
favourite
STORIES and
RHYMES

Published by Ladybird Books Ltd
A Penguin Company
Penguin Books Ltd, 80 Strand, London, WC2R 0RL, UK
Penguin Books Australia Ltd, Camberwell, Victoria, Australia
Penguin Books (NZ) Ltd, 67 Apollo Drive, Rosedale,
North Shore 0632, Auckland, New Zealand
(a division of Pearson New Zealand Ltd)

ISBN 978 1 40931 225 3
001 - 10 9 8 7 6 5 4 3 2 1

Printed in China

50

favourite
STORIES and
RHYMES

~ Contents ~

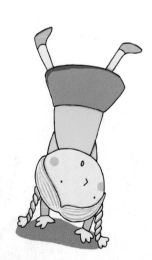

Festive Songs

Contents

Stories to Share
Pony Stories to Share

Monster Stories to Share

Pirate Stories to Share

Princess Stories to Share

Belle's Big Idea

Written by Fiona Munro ★ *Illustrated by* Marcin Piwowarski

WHEN BELLE WAS a little girl, she lived in a friendly village in Jamaica. She had lots of friends and spent happy days playing and having fun.

One day, Belle's mother made the long journey to England, to care for a sick auntie, and Belle went too. They liked England and decided to stay. Many years later, Belle got married and had two children of her own, Christopher and Mary.

Living in a big city like London, Belle's children couldn't easily run around and make friends. It was very different to Belle's life in Jamaica.

When Christopher started school, Mary had no one to play with, and no one to come to her birthday party!

So Belle talked to other mothers outside the school gates. She asked them to help her set up a playgroup, where young children could play and learn together. It was a difficult job starting up the first one, but Belle and her new friends never gave up. Luckily, a nice local church allowed the new playgroup to use their hall.

Belle's playgroup was so popular she thought children in other parts of the country might want to join one just like it.
She wrote a letter to a newspaper called *The Guardian* to tell people about it. In just one week, 150 people wrote to find out how to set up their own playgroup. Soon there were playgroups all over the country!

Today, across the country, there are grown ups who met their best friends at a playgroup just like Belle's. Maybe you will meet your best friend for life at your playgroup, too!

Thanks, Belle, for your big idea!

Rhymes
to Share

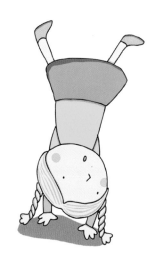

Illustrated by
Miriam Latimer ★ Virginia Allyn ★
Siobhan Harrison ★ Kanako Usui ★ Fernando Luiz ★
Natascia Ugliano ★ Ook Hallbjorn ★ Andrew Rowland ★
Kirsteen Harris-Jones ★ Holly Surplice

Teddy bear, Teddy bear

Teddy bear, teddy bear, turn around,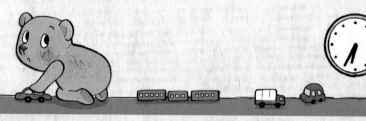

Teddy bear, teddy bear, touch the ground.

Teddy bear, teddy bear,
      climb the stairs,

Teddy bear, teddy bear, say your prayers.

Teddy bear, teddy bear,
      turn out the light,

Teddy bear, teddy bear, say goodnight.

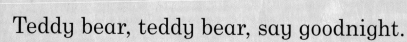

Ring-a-ring o'-roses

Ring-a-ring o' roses,
A pocket full of posies,
A-tishoo! A-tishoo!
We all fall down.

There was an Old Woman who Lived in a Shoe

There was an old woman
Who lived in a shoe,
She had so many children
She didn't know what to do;
She gave them some broth
Without any bread;
Then scolded them soundly
And sent them to bed.

Oranges and Lemons

"Oranges and lemons,"
Say the bells of St Clement's.

"You owe me five farthings,"
Say the bells of St Martin's.

"When will you pay me?"
Say the bells of Old Bailey.

"When I grow rich,"
Say the bells of Shoreditch.

"Pray, when will that be?"
Say the bells of Stepney.

"I'm sure I don't know,"
Says the great bell at Bow.

Here comes a candle
To light you to bed.

Here comes a chopper
To chop off your head.

23

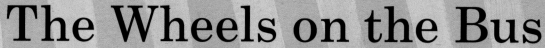

The Wheels on the Bus

The wheels on the bus go **round and round**,
Round and round, round and round.
The wheels on the bus go **round and round**,
All day long.

The wipers on the bus go **swish swish swish,**
Swish swish swish, swish swish swish.
The wipers on the bus go **swish swish swish,**
All day long.

25

Mary Had a Little Lamb

Mary had a little lamb,
Its fleece was white as snow;
And everywhere that Mary went
The lamb was sure to go.

It followed her to school one day,
That was against the rule;
It made the children laugh and play
To see a lamb at school.

Lavender's Blue

Lavender's blue, dilly, dilly,
Lavender's green;
When I am King, dilly, dilly,
You shall be Queen.

Roses are Red

Roses are red,
Violets are blue,
Sugar is sweet
And so are you.

Rub-a-dub-dub

Rub-a-dub-dub,
Three men in a tub
And how do you think they got there?
The butcher, the baker,
The candlestick-maker,
They all jumped out of a rotten potato;
'Twas enough to make a man stare.

Simple Simon

Simple Simon met a pieman
Going to the fair;
Said Simple Simon to the pieman,
"Let me taste your ware."

Said the pieman to Simple Simon,
"Show me first your penny."
Said Simple Simon to the pieman,
"Indeed, I have not any."

Polly, Put the Kettle on

Polly, put the kettle on,
Polly, put the kettle on,
Polly, put the kettle on,
We'll all have tea.

Sukey, take it off again,
Sukey, take it off again,
Sukey, take it off again,
They've all gone away.

Pussy Cat, Pussy Cat

Pussy cat, Pussy cat,
Where have you been?
"I've been to London
To visit the Queen."
Pussy cat, Pussy cat,
What did you there?

'I frightened a little mouse

under her chair."

One, Two, Buckle my Shoe

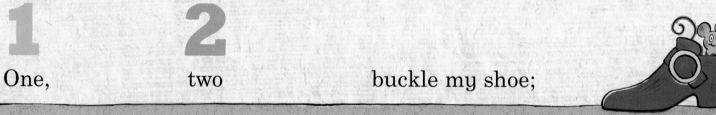

1 **2**

One, two buckle my shoe;

3 **4**

Three, four, knock at the door;

5 **6**

Five, six, pick up sticks;

7 **8**

Seven, eight, lay them straight;

9 **10**

Nine, ten a big fat hen!

Mary, Mary, Quite Contrary

Mary, Mary, quite contrary,
How does your garden grow?
With silver bells and cockle shells,
And pretty maids all in a row!

There was a Crooked Man

There was a crooked man,
And he walked a crooked mile.
He found a crooked sixpence
Against a crooked stile.
He bought a crooked cat,
Which caught a crooked mouse,
And they all lived together
In a little crooked house.

34

This Little Piggy went to Market

This little piggy went to market,

This little piggy stayed at home.

This little piggy had roast beef,

This little piggy had none.

This little piggy cried,
"Wee-wee-wee," all the way home.

Jack and Jill

Jack and Jill went up the hill,
To fetch a pail of water.
Jack fell down and broke his crown,
And Jill came tumbling after.

Little Bo-Peep

Little Bo-Peep has lost her sheep,
And doesn't know where to find them.
Leave them alone, and they'll come home,
Bringing their tails behind them.

Old Mother Hubbard

Old Mother Hubbard
Went to the cupboard
To fetch her poor dog a bone.
But when she got there
The cupboard was bare,
And so the poor dog had none.

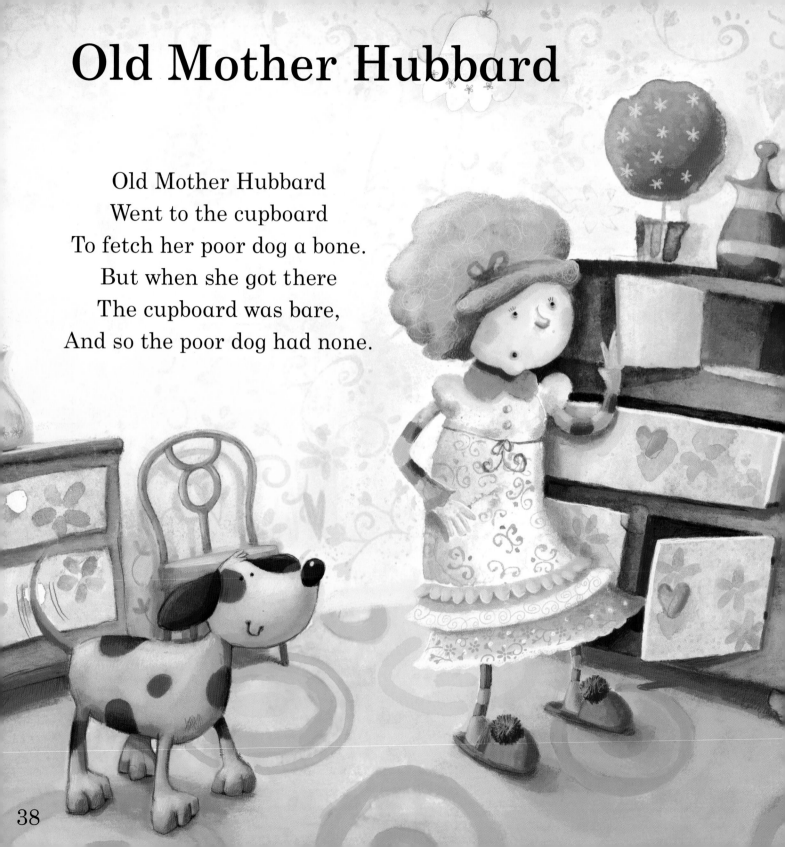

Tom, Tom, the Piper's Son

Tom, Tom, the piper's son,
Stole a pig and away did run;
The pig was eat
And Tom was beat,
And Tom went howling
Down the street.

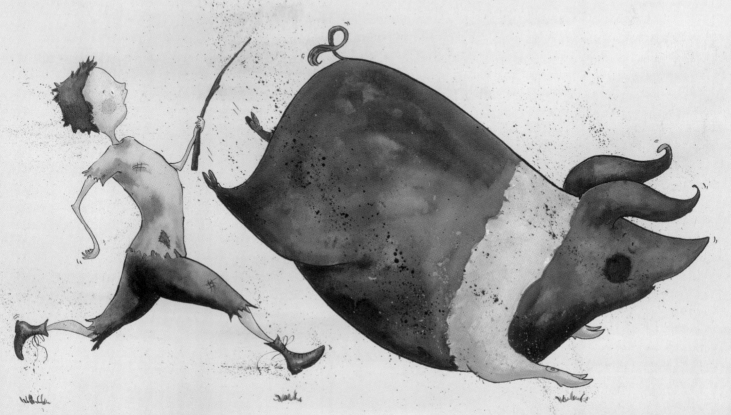

The Grand Old Duke of York

Oh, the grand old Duke of York,
He had ten thousand men.
He marched them up to the top of the hill,
And he marched them down again.

And when they were up, they were up,
And when they were down, they were down,
And when they were only halfway up,
They were neither up nor down!

One, Two, Three, Four, Five

One, two, three, four, five
Once I caught a fish alive,
Six, seven, eight, nine, ten,
Then I let it go again.
Why did you let it go?
Because it bit my finger so.
Which finger did it bite?
This little finger on the right.

Girls and Boys Come out to Play

Girls and boys come out to play,
The moon is shining bright as day.
Leave your supper and leave your sleep,
And come with your playfellows into the street.
Come with a whoop and come with a call,
Come with a good will or not at all.

Wee Willie Winkie

Wee Willie Winkie
Runs through the town,
Upstairs and downstairs
In his nightgown.
Rapping at the window,
Crying through the lock,
"Are the children all in bed?
For now it's eight o'clock!"

Good Night

Lullaby and good night, mummy's delight,
Bright angels around my darling shall stand.
They will guard you from harms,
You shall wake in my arms.
They will guard you from harms,
You shall wake in my arms.

Festive Songs

Illustrated by
Miriam Latimer ★ Simona Sanfilippo,
Nicola Evans ★ Giuditta Gaviraghi ★ Alik Arzoumanian

Jingle Bells

Dashing through the snow
In a one-horse open sleigh,
O'er the fields we go,
Laughing all the way.
Bells on bob-tail ring,
Making spirits bright.
What fun it is to ride and sing
a sleighing song tonight.

Jingle bells, jingle bells,
jingle all the way.
Oh, what fun it is to ride
in a one-horse open sleigh.
Jingle bells, jingle bells,
jingle all the way.
Oh, what fun it is to ride
in a one-horse open sleigh.

49

We Wish You a Merry Christmas

We wish you a merry Christmas,
We wish you a merry Christmas,
We wish you a merry Christmas
and a happy New Year!

Good tidings we bring
For you and your kin,
We wish you a merry Christmas
and a happy New Year!

Now bring us some figgy pudding,
Now bring us some figgy pudding,
Now bring us some figgy pudding,
Now bring some to us here.

Good tidings we bring
For you and your kin,
We wish you a merry Christmas
and a happy New Year!

We won't go until we get it,
We won't go until we get it,
We won't go until we get it,
So bring some right here!

Good tidings we bring
For you and your kin,
We wish you a merry Christmas
and a happy New Year!

We all like a figgy pudding,
We all like a figgy pudding,
So bring us some figgy pudding,
With all its good cheer!

Good tidings we bring
For you and your kin,
We wish you a merry Christmas
and a happy New Year!

53

The Twelve Days of Christmas

On the first day of Christmas
my true love sent to me,
a partridge in a pear tree.

On the second day of Christmas
my true love sent to me,
two turtledoves
and a partridge in a pear tree.

On the third day of Christmas
my true love sent to me,
three French hens,
two turtledoves
and a partridge in a pear tree.

On the fourth day of Christmas
my true love sent to me,
four calling birds,
three French hens...

On the fifth day of Christmas
my true love sent to me,
five gold rings,
four calling birds...

On the sixth day of Christmas
my true love sent to me,
six geese a-laying,
five gold rings...

On the seventh day of Christmas
my true love sent to me,
seven swans a-swimming,
six geese a-laying...

On the eighth day of Christmas
my true love sent to me,
eight maids a-milking,
seven swans a-swimming...

On the ninth day of Christmas
my true love sent to me,
nine ladies dancing,
eight maids a-milking...

On the tenth day of Christmas
my true love sent to me,
ten lords a-leaping,
nine ladies dancing...

On the eleventh day of Christmas
my true love sent to me,
eleven pipers piping,
ten lords a-leaping...

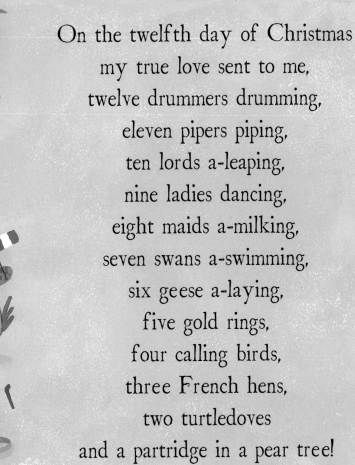

On the twelfth day of Christmas
my true love sent to me,
twelve drummers drumming,
eleven pipers piping,
ten lords a-leaping,
nine ladies dancing,
eight maids a-milking,
seven swans a-swimming,
six geese a-laying,
five gold rings,
four calling birds,
three French hens,
two turtledoves
and a partridge in a pear tree!

Away in a Manger

Away in a manger, no crib for a bed,
The little Lord Jesus laid down his sweet head.
The stars in the bright sky looked down where he lay,
The little Lord Jesus asleep on the hay.

The cattle are lowing, the baby awakes,
But little Lord Jesus no crying he makes.
I love thee, Lord Jesus! Look down from the sky,
And stay by my bedside till morning is nigh.

Be near me, Lord Jesus; I ask thee to stay
Close by me forever, and love me, I pray.
Bless all the dear children in thy tender care,
And fit us for heaven, to live with thee there.

59

Deck the Halls

Deck the halls with boughs of holly,
Fa-la-la-la-la, la-la-la-la.
'Tis the season to be jolly,
Fa-la-la-la-la, la-la-la-la.

Don we now our gay apparel,
Fa-la-la-la-la, la-la-la-la.
Troll the ancient Yuletide carol,
Fa-la-la-la-la, la-la-la-la.

See the blazing Yule before us,
Fa-la-la-la-la, la-la-la-la.
Strike the harp and join the chorus,
Fa-la-la-la-la, la-la-la-la.

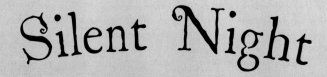

Silent Night

Silent night! Holy night!
All is calm, all is bright.
Round yon Virgin Mother and Child!
Holy Infant, so tender and mild,
Sleep in heavenly peace!
Sleep in heavenly peace!

Silent night! Holy night!
Shepherds quake at the sight!
Glories stream from heaven afar,
Heavenly hosts sing, 'Alleluia!'
Christ, the Saviour, is born!
Christ, the Saviour, is born!

Silent night! Holy night!
Son of God, love's pure light!
Radiant beams from thy holy face
With the dawn of redeeming grace,
Jesus, Lord, at thy birth!
Jesus, Lord, at thy birth!

The Holly and the Ivy

The holly and the ivy,
When they are both full grown,
Of all the trees that are in the wood,
The holly bears the crown.

O, the rising of the sun
And the running of the deer,
The playing of the merry organ,
Sweet singing in the choir.

65

Pony Stories
to Share

Written by Marie Birkinshaw ★ *Illustrated by* Caroline Freake

Speedy Goes Shopping

Speedy the pony loves galloping as fast as she can. That's how she got her name – Speedy, the fastest little pony ever. In her hurry, Speedy often gets things wrong or gets in the way. But Farmer Henry doesn't mind. He knows that Speedy is only trying to help.

One spring day, Farmer Henry was very busy with the lambs. "This is hot work, Speedy," he said. He wiped his eyes and mopped his head.

Speedy galloped away. She filled a bucket full of water for Farmer Henry.
Zoom! Back she came. But most of the water had spilled!
"Thank you, Speedy," said Farmer Henry, kindly. "I'm sorry, but I don't have an apple for you today and I don't have time to go shopping. Perhaps you can help?"
Farmer Henry gave Speedy a shopping list. Speedy didn't waste a second. She galloped to fetch her mum.

First they went to the bakery. Speedy showed the baker the list.
The baker helped to fill up their bags.
Next, the two ponies visited the dairy. While Honey looked for yoghurts
and cheese, Speedy decided to speed things up by choosing some eggs.

Whoops! Last of all, the ponies bought some apples. The shopping was all done. Speedy galloped home, in a hurry!

Farmer Henry patted Honey's mane and handed an apple to Speedy. "Well done, Speedy," he said. "That's the fastest shopping ever!"

Speedy to the Rescue

It was a hot summer's day. Farmer Henry was working hard, and Speedy was racing around, doing her best to help.

The farmer's two children, Tom and Lucy, came to see them.

They were pulling their go-karts.

"We're going to meet some friends to have a race," said Lucy.

"Why don't you go along too, Speedy?" said Farmer Henry. Speedy was so excited that she galloped all around the field!

Three... two... one... the go-karts set off down the hill. Lucy took the lead, but she was soon overtaken by her friend Jamie. Tom caught the edge of the kerb and came to a stop. **Crunch!** Luckily, no one was hurt.

But where was Speedy? Right at the front of course! Fast little ponies love races.

But suddenly – **ker-crunch!** Jamie lost control and headed straight for the pond... going faster and faster!

"Speedy to the rescue," neighed the fastest little pony.

Speedy galloped down the hill faster and faster.
"Help!" Jamie shouted.
Speedy galloped as quickly as she could after him. The go-kart turned off
the path. But just as Jamie hit the water, Speedy put on a final burst of
speed and overtook him. Speedy pushed Jamie's go-kart to one side away
from the water.

But she couldn't stop herself in time and Speedy landed in the water with a great big **SPLASH!**

"Three cheers for Speedy," shouted the children. **"HIP, HIP, HOORAY!"**

"You're the fastest and the wettest pony ever," laughed Tom and Lucy. Speedy gave them a cheeky smile. Then she shook the water out of her mane, and gave everyone a soaking.

Speedy Wins the Race

It was the day of the village show. Farmer Henry only had a few more jobs to do before he was ready to set off. Speedy had been racing about helping him all morning.

Finally, they got to the stables. Speedy picked up brushes, combs and ribbons and took them to Farmer Henry. He was getting her mum, Honey, ready for the prettiest pony competition.

He led Honey out to the truck.

After so much helping and running around, Speedy suddenly felt very tired. She snuggled down in the straw of the stable and fell asleep.

Meanwhile, Farmer Henry finished loading up the truck.

"Ponies... sheep... vegetables... Yes, everything's ready," said Farmer Henry.

He closed the truck door and put on his seat belt. **Brrrm!** He started up the engine and set off.

The sound of the engine woke Speedy. She ran out into the yard and saw Farmer Henry's truck heading away down the road. "Wait for me!" she neighed. But Farmer Henry couldn't hear her. Speedy galloped after the truck. She took a short cut across the field and jumped over the stream. She carried on galloping as fast as she could. Soon, she reached the showground. The sound of loud cheers and clapping made her run even faster.

BANG! A race was just starting. But Speedy didn't notice.
The little pony just galloped faster and faster...
She didn't stop galloping... until she reached the finish line! Honey and Farmer Henry rushed over to meet her.

"There you are, Speedy!" said Farmer Henry.

What a day! Honey had won the prettiest pony prize, and Farmer Henry's vegetables were some of the biggest and best. And of course, Speedy had won the race!

"Well done, Speedy," said Farmer Henry.

"You really are the fastest little pony ever!"

Monster Stories
to Share

Written by Rebecca Lim ★ *Illustrated by* Caroline Freake

Fernando Makes a Mess

Fernando Monster lived in a big, monster house with his parents, Mr and Mrs Monster, and his sister, Betty Monster.

Fernando went to monster school, and he did his monster homework, and he played nicely with all the other little monsters.

"What a good little monster you are!" said his mum, proudly.

One day, Fernando decided to do finger-painting. His neat and tidy sister, Betty, was doing her neat and tidy jigsaw. Fernando made a lovely squiggly picture.

Splat! Whoops! Fernando knocked over the paint pots.

Then Fernando went to hang up his painting. **Squish! Squelch!** Fernando left a trail of squidgy red footprints on the floor. Fernando was quite a messy monster, wasn't he?

But Fernando wasn't finished. He decided to do just one more finger painting.

"I'm not going to just use my fingers, that's boring!" said Fernando, the messy monster. So what else did Fernando use?

His nose!

Now there was paint all over the floor... and all over Fernando.

What a mess! "I'll just wash off this paint..." said Fernando. And he found a lovely muddy puddle outside to jump in.

Was Fernando messy enough by now? No, he wasn't. One puddle jump is never enough for a messy monster! **Split! Splat!** Pretty soon, Fernando was covered in paint and mud.

Fernando went squelching happily back into the kitchen. There never was a messier little monster. Fernando just couldn't help it!

"Oh, Fernando!" said his mum, smiling. "You really are the messiest monster ever!"

A Visit to the Park

Fernando Monster was very excited. Daddy was taking him and his friends, Alfie and George, to the park.

"Try not to let them get too messy today," said Mummy.

"Yes, dear," said Daddy.

Fernando liked everything about Monster Park, but most of all he loved it after the rain, when lots of muddy puddles sprang up everywhere.

What was it Fernando liked so much about muddy puddles? He loved splashing and jumping in them.

"Now, we're trying not to get too messy today," said his dad.

"Yes, Daddy," said Fernando. He really tried to be a good little monster. And then Fernando rushed off to play. Daddy Monster sat down to read the newspaper.

What was the first thing the three monster friends did? Jump in the muddy puddles, of course!

"Yippee!" they yelled. They were soaking wet, but Daddy didn't notice.

"What about the sandpit next?" he said.

Fernando and his friends made a big sandcastle, and covered each other in the sand, and rolled about. What fun it was, being muddy and sandy monsters!

Daddy was still reading his newspaper.

"Time for a monster slide," he said, without looking up.

What do you think was waiting for the three friends at the bottom of the slide? A lovely, big, monster puddle to land in!

"Time to go home," said Daddy.

And then he noticed the muddy monsters.

"Hmm," said Daddy. But he was smiling. He knew Fernando just couldn't help it.

At home, Daddy was still smiling.

"One happy, messy little monster," he said. Mummy laughed.

"Oh, Fernando!" she said. "You really are the messiest monster ever!"

"Yes," said Fernando proudly. "And this time it was all Daddy's idea!"

SPLISH!

Fernando's Surprise

On Sundays, Mummy Monster took her little monsters to see
their grandparents.
"Have fun," she said and gave them a big hug.
Grandma and Grandpa's monster house was called Magnificent Manor.
It had a big front door and six chimneys! Grandma Monster even
had a pet sheep, to keep the grass neat in the garden.

CRASH!

"I must try not to make a mess," said Fernando. Then he ran into the house and up the stairs, past a big vase of flowers and... what do you think happened next?

Crash! Oh dear! Fernando fell over. He knocked over the vase. Flowers flew everywhere. Water splashed on the carpet. What a mess!

Crash! Smash! Oh dear! Fernando fell over again. He knocked over an umbrella stand. Umbrellas flew everywhere. What a terrible mess!

"Whoops!" said Fernando, the messy monster. He picked himself up. He turned around, and... **Clatter! Boom!** He knocked over a statue. One, two, three messes!

"Never mind! Let's go and get the dustpan and brush," said Grandpa, kindly.

Grandpa and Fernando walked into the kitchen... and there was Grandma, making ice cream with Betty. There was ice cream everywhere!

It was all over the table and all over Grandma.

"Tee-hee!" said Grandma. "What a mess!"

As they ate their delicious ice creams, Grandma said, "When I was little, I was the messiest monster ever. Sometimes, I still make a mess – I just can't help it!"

What a surprise! Fernando laughed. He laughed so hard he fell forward... and what do you think happened next?

Pirate Stories
to Share

Written by Marie Birkinshaw ★ *Illustrated by* Caroline Freake

Busy Pirate Billy

Busy Pirate Billy lives with his mum, Captain June, his dad, First Mate Ben, Spud, the ship's cook and Seaweed, the ship's cat. Their home is an amazing pirate ship, called the Goldrush. Every day they sail the seas in search of buried treasure.

Billy's best friend is Seaweed. Busy Pirate Billy is always busy on the Goldrush helping Captain June and having fun. Seaweed likes to sleep in the sun.

Early one morning, Billy got out of bed. He put on his pirate clothes, and said, "Come on, Seaweed. There's work to do. But we must be quiet or we'll wake the crew."

He took out his telescope and looked at the sea... But the ship wasn't bobbing up and down as it should be. It was rushing towards the rocks at great speed!

Straightaway, the busy little pirate took charge. **Ding, ding!** He rang the ship's bell to wake everyone up.

"It's too early, Pirate Billy. Go back to sleep!" First Mate Ben yawned, and closed his eyes again.

Ding, ding! "We've lost the anchor!" Billy shouted. "All hands on deck!"

Captain June raced to the wheel and set the ship straight in the water.

"Well done, my busy Billy," said Captain June. "You saved the Goldrush!"

Billy grinned happily.

Spud and Billy got busy making the breakfast for the crew, and of course, Seaweed ate at the table, too.

The Pirate Games

Today was the Junior Pirate Games. All the pirate families met up for an exciting day of games for the young pirates. Billy and Seaweed had been busy practising for weeks. As the Goldrush steered towards the island where the games were held, the busy little pirate watched through his telescope.

"Come on, Seaweed," Billy said, "we've lots to do."

The first event of the Junior Pirate Games was diving for gold coins. Billy wore his lucky diving mask, but it started to come loose and filled with water. Seaweed dived in and tried to help, but his paw got caught in Billy's hair. Billy came fifth.

The second event was ship steering skills in the bay. "I should be good at this!" said Billy. But his Captain's hat came down over his eyes and he couldn't see properly, so Billy came fourth.

The next event was a treasure hunt where Billy had to find ten gold coins and put them in a chest.

Billy started to dig. He found eight gold coins, an old boot and a crisp packet. He came third.

Play sword fighting followed. Swords flashed and metal clashed. Seaweed went to find somewhere to sleep. The busy little pirate did well and came second.

At last it was time for the final game – deck cleaning. When the judges checked the boards, Billy's were the cleanest of all. They were so shiny that Seaweed could use them as a mirror. He came first! At the end of the day, Billy was the only junior pirate to finish all the events. Billy won the prize of the The Busiest Pirate Ever! Even Seaweed got a prize for eating the most fish!

Busy Pirate Billy and the Mysterious Map

It was spring-cleaning day on the Goldrush. At sunrise, busy little Pirate Billy and Seaweed rang the ship's bell. Everyone groaned and gathered on the top deck.

"Right, crew," said Captain June. "It's time to scrub and clean. Make the Goldrush as spotless as it's ever been."

All the crew set to work.

Billy and Seaweed went to the very bottom of the ship. This was where the barrels of drinking water were kept.

Atishoo! Atishoo! It was dusty but they soon got to work. Billy's broom got caught between two barrels and he had to pull hard to get it free. **Pop!** Out came the broom knocking Billy and Seaweed over.

"Look, Seaweed! It's a map!" Billy shouted.

The busy little pirate and the ship's cat took the map straight to Captain June.

"Wow!" she said. "I haven't seen this before." Seaweed pointed to the X with his paw.

"Come on, Seaweed," Billy said. "Let's get busy! I wonder what we'll find if we follow the clues."

The map led them to an old, rusty key.

"Will it fit this chest?" said Billy. "Let me see." Billy clutched the key and put it in the lock.

Inside the chest was a dusty old recipe for Shiver Me Timbers ice cream!
Spud, the ship's cook, was very happy.
"Oh thank you, Billy! Let's make ice cream!" Spud exclaimed.

Princess Stories
to Share

Written by Rebecca Lim ★ *Illustrated by* Caroline Freake

The Hungry Dragon

Brave Princess Arabella lived in a big castle, next to a village. She always wore a crown and a pretty dress.

One day, Arabella was out riding her royal pony when she heard a great rumpus.

So she jumped off her horse, climbed the tallest tower in the castle, and looked out. She saw a fierce, fire-breathing dragon!

The fierce, fire-breathing dragon looked hungry! The dragon's tummy rumbled so much the ground shook.

"Dragon!" screamed the villagers, and they hid anywhere they could. But they needn't have worried as this was not a people-eating sort of dragon.

"Goodness me!" Arabella said crossly as she watched the dragon take food from the village stalls. "What a naughty, greedy dragon!"

So, brave Princess Arabella went in search of the dragon. She found it frightening Mrs Honey at the cake shop. But Princess Arabella wasn't afraid of the fierce, fire-breathing dragon. Arabella had something to tell it!

Arabella pulled on the dragon's tail to get its attention.

"Hello!" said Arabella. "How do you do?"

The hungry dragon was far too surprised to be fierce.

Arabella sat down to share a plate of delicious cakes with the dragon. And when all the cakes were eaten up, do you know what that fierce dragon said? "Thank you!"

The Magical Forest

Behind the castle where Princess Arabella lived was a magical forest.
One day, the villagers heard a terrible wailing sound coming from the
trees. Nobody wanted to go into the forest! Nobody except... a brave little
princess. One morning, at breakfast, Princess Arabella said, "I'm going for
a walk in the forest today. I want to see what's making that terrible noise."

"But sweetie-pie..." protested her poor mother, Queen Louise.

It was no use. Princess Arabella hardly ever changed her mind.

She packed her pyjamas and toothbrush into a bag. "Just in case," said Arabella, "I decide to camp out."

"Camp out? Now, my little angel..." began her anxious father, King Lewis.

"Don't worry, Dad!" called Arabella as she marched out of the castle, towards the dark forest. Tall trees hung over her... and then she disappeared from view.

Arabella took two steps into the forest.

The moaning was so loud that she had to cover her ears. In the gloom, she saw an unhappy witch looking miserable.

"Hello, witch. Why are you making that terrible noise? Do you have a toothache?" said brave Arabella.

The witch nodded miserably.

"Wait here," Arabella said to the tearful witch. She went to fetch the royal dentist. He pulled out the witch's sore tooth and gave the witch a new toothbrush!

Even though the moaning stopped coming from the forest, still nobody liked to visit. Except Arabella, the bravest princess ever. She often went to make sure the witch was brushing her teeth!

Arabella Saves the Day

One special day the circus came to town. A big tent was put up, right next to the castle where Princess Arabella lived.

"Roll up! Roll up!" bellowed the ringmaster.

Everyone came to see the amazing circus. Trapeze artists flew through the air. Acrobats tumbled. The crowd cheered.

Princess Arabella watched from the royal box. A graceful ballerina danced across the tightrope, way up high. Arabella clapped her hands, "Wow!" she said. "I wish I could do that!"

Two funny clowns bounced into the ring, and the crowd cheered happily. But Arabella was watching the trapeze artists, swinging high up above their heads.

Then suddenly, Princess Arabella noticed something. Someone was in trouble! It was a trapeze artist, all tangled in a rope way up high.

Brave Princess Arabella went to the rescue! Quick as a flash, a clown helped Arabella to climb up the ladder and free the trapeze artist. "Hooray!" screamed the crowd.

Even though she was now dangling up in the air beside the trapeze artist, Arabella was not worried at all! The trapeze artist helped her onto the swing and she swung to and fro. The crowd clapped and cheered.

"That was the best fun ever!" said Arabella, as King Lewis and Queen Louise gave her a big cuddle.

"And you're the bravest princess ever," said her parents proudly.

The circus ringmaster bellowed, "Three cheers for the bravest princess ever! Hip, Hip, Hooray! Hip, Hip Hooray! Hip, Hip Hooray!"

Little
Red
Riding Hood

BASED ON A TRADITIONAL FOLK TALE

retold by Mandy Ross ★ *illustrated by* Anja Rieger

Once upon a time there was a small girl called Little Red Riding Hood. She lived with her parents beside a deep, dark forest.

...a big, bad wolf.

"Grandmother's poorly," said Little Red Riding
Hood's mother one day. "Please take her this cake.
But don't stop on the way!"

So Little Red Riding Hood set off through the
deep, dark forest. She looked all around.
There wasn't a sound.
Then who should she meet but...

...the big, bad wolf.
"Good day, my dear," growled the wolf with
a big, bad smile. "What are you doing here?"

She looks delicious!

"I'm going to Grandmother's to take her a cake," replied Little Red Riding Hood.

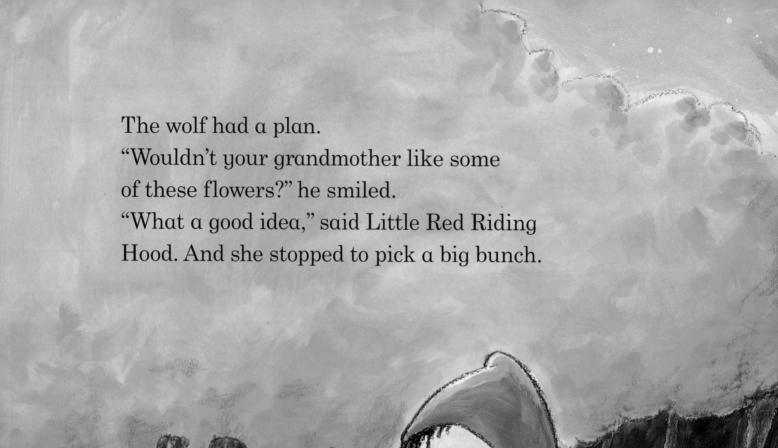

The wolf had a plan.
"Wouldn't your grandmother like some
of these flowers?" he smiled.
"What a good idea," said Little Red Riding
Hood. And she stopped to pick a big bunch.

Meanwhile, the wolf sped ahead through the deep, dark forest. At last he arrived at...

...Grandmother's cottage.
"I'm **HUNGRY**," thought the big, bad wolf, licking his lips. And he knock-knock-knocked at the door.

"Hello, Grandmother," growled the wolf.
"It's Little Red Riding Hood."
"That sounds more like the big, bad wolf,"
thought Grandmother, and she crept quickly
under the bed.

The wolf went in. He looked all around,
but there wasn't a sound.
Then his tummy rumbled.

"No one's here," he grumbled. "Never mind.
Little Red Riding Hood will be along soon."

It's dusty!
I mustn't sneeze.

Quickly the wolf put on Grandmother's dressing gown and nightcap. Then he hopped into bed and pretended to nap. "Heh! Heh! Heh!" he snarled. "Little Red Riding Hood will never know it's me!"

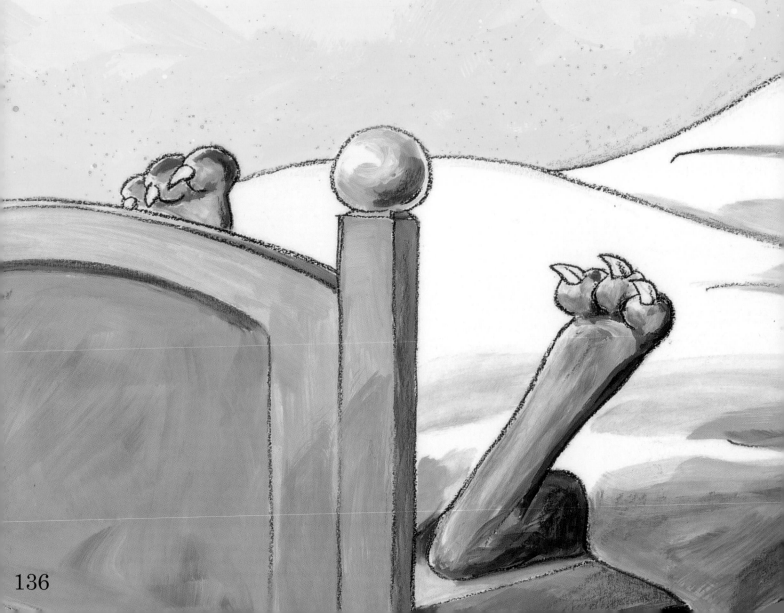

Soon Little Red Riding Hood knock-knock-
knocked at the door.
"Hello, Grandmother," she called.
"It's Little Red Riding Hood."

"Come in, my dear," growled the wolf.
Little Red Riding Hood opened the door.
"Oh, Grandmother!" she gasped...

"...What big ears you have!"

"All the better to hear you with, my dear," growled the wolf.

"And Grandmother, what big eyes you have!"

"All the better to see you with, my dear," growled the wolf.

"And Grandmother, what big teeth you have!"

"All the better to...

141

...GOBBLE YOU UP!" roared the wolf.
But as he leapt out of bed, Grandmother's
nightcap flopped right over his head.

I can't see anything!

"Quick! Down here, dear!" whispered
Grandmother, and she pulled Little Red
Riding Hood under the bed.

Just then, a woodcutter passed by the cottage. He heard a growling and howling...

and he dashed inside.
With one **SWISH!** of his axe he killed the big bad wolf.

144

The woodcutter looked all around.
But there wasn't a sound. And then...

...out crept Little Red Riding Hood
and Grandmother from under the bed.

And Little Red Riding Hood said,
"Mother was right. I'll *never* stop again
on my way through the forest!"

The Gingerbread Man

BASED ON A TRADITIONAL FOLK TALE

retold by Alan MacDonald ★ *illustrated by* Anja Rieger

One morning a baker said to his wife,
"Today I'll bake a gingerbread man.
He'll look just right in our shop window."

So the baker made a gingerbread man
and put him in the oven. Before long they
heard a noise. A little voice began to shout,

"Open the door! Let me out!"

Let me
out!

As soon as the baker opened the oven door,

the gingerbread man jumped down to the floor...

I'm off!

and ran right out of the shop.

The baker and his wife chased him down the street, shouting, "Come back here, little ginger feet!"
But the gingerbread man just ran and ran, singing,

He hadn't gone far when...

...a hungry boy joined the chase calling,
"Come back here, little ginger face!"
But the gingerbread man just ran and
ran, singing,

...a hungry cow who said,
"Come back here, little ginger head!"
But the gingerbread man just ran and
ran, singing,

"Run, run as fast as you can,

It wasn't long before he met...

...a hungry horse, neighing, "Come back here, little ginger paws!" But the gingerbread man just ran and ran, singing,

"Run, run, as fast as you can, You can't catch me, I'm the gingerbread man!"

Behind him chased the horse, the cow, the boy, the baker and his wife.

In the woods hid a hungry fox. He called,
"What's the hurry, little ginger socks?"
But the gingerbread man just ran and
ran, singing,

"Run, run, as fast as you can,
You can't catch me, I'm the gingerbread man!"

No time for that!

He was just thinking how clever he was,
when...

...he came to a wide, wide river.
The gingerbread man stopped. He needed to
think. Up crept the fox and said with a wink,

"Jump onto my tail and I'll take you across."
The gingerbread man thanked the sly fox
and he jumped onto his bushy tail.

The fox started to swim across the wide, wide river. Very soon he said, "Little gingerbread man, you're too heavy for my tail. Why not jump onto my red, red back?"

So the gingerbread man jumped onto the fox's back.

Look out!

But soon the fox said, "Little gingerbread man, you're too heavy for my back. Why not hop onto my shiny, black nose?"

So the gingerbread man hopped
onto the fox's nose.

Just as they came near to the bank, the fox tossed back his head. And with a flick of his neck, he tossed the gingerbread man up, up, up in the air.

Then the gingerbread man fell

down, down, down...

SNAP! straight into the fox's gaping mouth.

And that was the end of the gingerbread man.

With a sly smile, the fox trotted home, singing,

"Run, run, as fast as you can,
But I caught you, little gingerbread man!"

173

Goldilocks
and the
Three Bears

BASED ON A TRADITIONAL FOLK TALE

retold by Nicola Baxter ★ *illustrated by* Liz Pichon

Deep in the forest lived three bears.

There was **BIG** Father Bear,

middle-sized Mother Bear,

and tiny little
Baby Bear.

Father Bear had a **BIG** voice. Mother Bear
had a middle-sized voice. Baby Bear had a tiny
little voice. You could only just hear it.

Bright and early one morning, Mother Bear
was busy making breakfast.
"We'll enjoy our porridge even more if we have
a little walk first," said Father Bear.

But while the bears were walking, so was
someone else. It was a little girl called...

...Goldilocks.
She had golden hair, and her cheeks
were rosy. But little Goldilocks was
rather nosy!

When she saw the house, with the door open wide, that naughty little girl walked right inside!

Goldilocks was feeling peckish. There on the
table she saw three bowls of porridge,
so she picked up a spoon to have a taste.

The first bowl of porridge was much too hot.
The second bowl was much too lumpy!
But, "Mmmmm!" The third little bowl
was just right... and suddenly it was
absolutely empty!

One... two... three bowls.

Feeling rather full and sleepy, Goldilocks looked for a chair. How many do you think were standing there?

The first chair was much too hard.
The second chair was much too soft!
But the third little chair was just right—
for a baby bear. Goldilocks sat down and...

...CRASH! She smashed the little chair.

Goldilocks felt tired and cross after such a bruising bump. She quickly hurried up the stairs and peeked into the...

...bedroom.
There she saw a **BIG** bed, a middle-sized bed and a tiny little cosy bed.

The first bed was much too hard.
The second bed was much too soft!
But, "Mmmmm!" The third little bed
was just right...

...for a snooz-z-z-z-z-z-z-z-z-z-z-z-z-z-z-ze.

Meanwhile on the forest track, the three
bears were coming back.
They noticed right away that things
were wrong.

"Someone's been eating my porridge!"
growled Father Bear.
"Someone's been eating my porridge!"
said Mother Bear.

"Someone's been eating my porridge,"
squeaked Baby Bear, "and they've eaten it
all up!"

"Someone's been sitting in my chair!" growled
Father Bear.
"Someone's been sitting in my chair!"
said Mother Bear.

"Someone's been sitting in my chair, too," sobbed Baby Bear. He was the saddest bear of all. There was nothing left of his little chair.

Quietly on their furry paws, the bears crept slowly up the stairs.

"Someone's been sleeping in my bed!"
grunted Father Bear.
"Someone's been sleeping in my bed!"
said Mother Bear.
"Someone's been sleeping in my bed," squeaked
Baby Bear...

"...and she's still there!"
Baby Bear's tiny voice woke Goldilocks.
She opened one eye... and then the other...

Then she leapt out of bed, ran out of
the house, and never went back.
And what's more, after that Goldilocks
never had porridge for breakfast!

The Enormous Turnip

BASED ON A TRADITIONAL FOLK TALE

retold by Irene Yates ★ *illustrated by* Jan Lewis

Once, a man came out to his garden with his turnip seeds and his hoe. He dug and he delved and he set his seeds in a row.

He cared for his seeds and watered them well, and the turnip seeds began to ...

swell...

In a very few days came little green leaves.
They poked and they pushed and they
pointed. The man with the hoe rolled up
his sleeves ...

He plucked out the weeds and raked off the rubble. He didn't know there was going to be trouble.

At last the turnips began to grow. They got bigger and **bigger** and **bigger**. And the man with the hoe said, "So ... we'll have turnips for breakfast and lunch and for tea. And it's turnips for supper, too, thanks to me."

One of the turnips — the best of the lot —
began to take over the whole of his plot.

It grew bigger and bigger every day.
It was huge. It was vast. It was . . .

ENORMOUS!

The other poor turnips got out of its way.

The man was baffled but he kept on hoeing.
And the ENORMOUS turnip kept on growing.

The man thought it must be time at last
to pull the turnip, but it just stuck fast.

"Come and help heave!" called the man to
his wife.

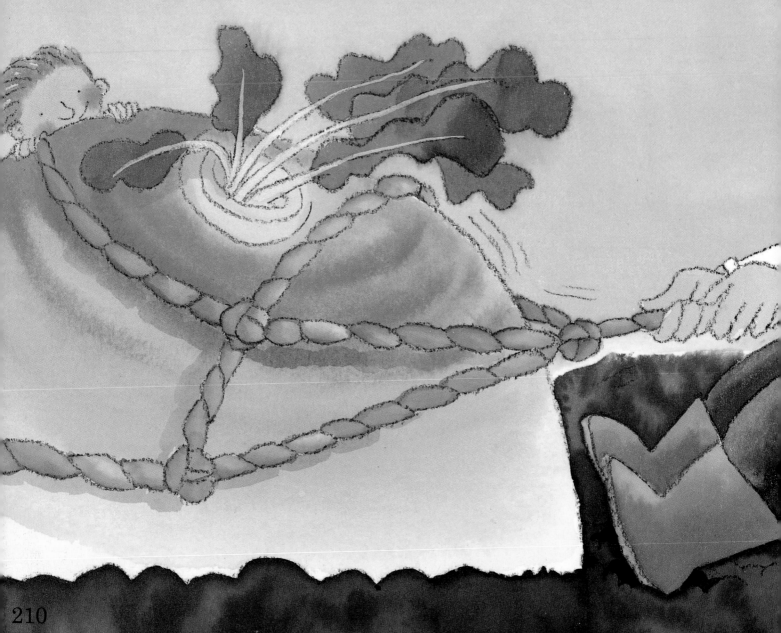

The man pulled the turnip and the wife pulled the man. But the ENORMOUS turnip just wouldn't budge!

Heave!

"Come and help heave!" called the wife to a boy.

The man pulled the turnip, the wife pulled the man, the boy pulled the wife.

All together!

But the ENORMOUS turnip just wouldn't budge!

"Come and help heave!" called the boy to a girl.

The man pulled the turnip, the wife pulled the man, the boy pulled the wife, the girl pulled the boy.

But the ENORMOUS turnip just wouldn't budge!

One, two, three . . . !

"Come and help heave!" called the girl
to a dog.

The man pulled the turnip, the wife pulled the
man, the boy pulled the wife, the girl pulled
the boy, the dog pulled the girl.

But the ENORMOUS turnip just
wouldn't budge!

Woof!

21

"Come and help heave!" called the dog to a cat.

The man pulled the turnip, the wife pulled the man, the boy pulled the wife, the girl pulled the boy, the dog pulled the girl, the cat pulled the dog.

Miaow!

But the ENORMOUS turnip just wouldn't budge!

"Come and help heave!" called the cat to
a mouse.

The man pulled the turnip, the wife pulled the man, the boy pulled the wife, the girl pulled the boy, the dog pulled the girl, the cat pulled the dog, the mouse pulled the cat and...

bump... bump!

Miaow!

223

Then it was turnip for breakfast and lunch
and for tea, and turnip for supper and . . .
oh, deary me!

Anyone for
seconds?

The turnip's so good that they can't get their fill and it's just so **ENORMOUS** they're eating it still!

Jack
and the
Beanstalk

BASED ON A TRADITIONAL FOLK TALE

retold by Iona Treahy ★ *illustrated by* Ruth Rivers

Once there was a boy called Jack who lived
with his mother. They were so poor that she
said to him one day, "We'll have to sell our
cow — it's the only way."

So Jack took the cow to market.

I'll miss you, Daisy.

On the way, Jack met a stranger.
"I'll give you five beans for that cow,"
she said. "They're magic beans..."
"Done!" said Jack. But when he got back...

"Five beans for our cow?" cried his mother.
And she threw them out of the window.

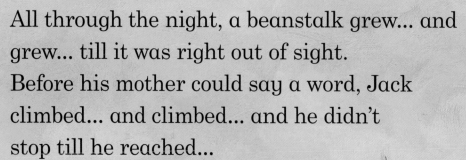

All through the night, a beanstalk grew... and
grew... till it was right out of sight.
Before his mother could say a word, Jack
climbed... and climbed... and he didn't
stop till he reached...

...the top. There Jack saw a giant castle.
He knock-knock-knocked, and a giantess
opened the door.
Inside, Jack could hear a **thumping** and
a **banging** and a **stamping** and a **crashing**.

What a noise!

"Quick," said the giantess. "Hide!
My husband is hungry!"

"Fee, fi, fo, fum! Watch out everyone, HERE I COME!" roared the giant.

The giant sat down for his supper. He ate
one hundred boiled potatoes, and one hundred
chocolate biscuits. And then, feeling a bit
happier, he got out his gold.

The giant started counting his coins,
but soon... he was snoozing.

Zzzzzzz...

Jack snatched the gold and *raced*
down the beanstalk.
"Gold!" cried Jack's mother when she saw
what he'd got. "We're not poor any more!"

But Jack wanted to go back up the beanstalk.
The next day he climbed...
and climbed... and he didn't stop till
he reached the top.

Inside the castle, Jack hid when he heard...

a **thumping** and a **banging** and a **stamping** and a **crashing**.

"Fee, fi, fo, fum!
Watch out everyone,
HERE I COME!" roared the giant.

The giant sat down for his supper. He ate
two hundred baked potatoes, and two hundred
jellies. And then, feeling a bit happier, he got out
his hen that laid golden eggs.

The hen started laying, but soon...
the giant was snoozing. Jack snatched
the hen and *raced* down
the beanstalk.

244

"Golden eggs from a golden hen!"
cried Jack's mother. "Now we'll
never be poor again!"

The next day, Jack climbed the beanstalk
once more.
"Fee, fi, fo, fum!
Watch out everyone,
HERE I COME!" roared the giant.

The giant sat down for his supper. He ate three hundred roast potatoes, and three hundred cream cakes. And then, feeling a bit happier, he got out his silver harp.

247

The harp sang him lullabies, and soon... the giant was snoozing. Jack snatched the harp and *raced* down the beanstalk.

But the harp called out, "Master! Master!"
The giant woke up and started to chase
after Jack.

"Bring the axe, Mother!" shouted Jack as he neared the ground. Then he chopped and he chopped and didn't stop till...

CRASH!

Down came the beanstalk and the giant.

And with the gold and the harp and the eggs
and the hen, Jack and his mother
were never poor again.

This special storybook of 50 stories and rhymes celebrates
the Pre-school Learning Alliance's 50th Birthday.

The Pre-school Learning Alliance continues Belle's legacy today.
14,000 members deliver high quality childcare and support to over
800,000 families every day in England.

You can find out more about the work we do at

www.pre-school.org.uk